Tested

by DIANA GALLAGHER

STONE ARCH BOOKS
a capstone imprint

CLAUDIA AND MONICA: FRESHMAN GIRLS
ARE PUBLISHED BY STONE ARCH BOOKS
A CAPSTONE IMPRINT
1710 ROE CREST DRIVE
NORTH MANKATO, MN 56003

LIBRARY OF CONGRESS CATALOGING-IN-PUBLICATION DATA

GALLAGHER, DIANA G.
  TESTED / BY DIANA G. GALLAGHER.
      P. CM. -- (CLAUDIA AND MONICA, FRESHMAN GIRLS)
  SUMMARY: CLAUDIA AND MONICA ARE BOTH HAVING BOYFRIEND
TROUBLE—WILL THEY BE ABLE TO SET THINGS RIGHT WITH BRAD AND
RORY, OR WILL A LACK OF TRUST TEAR THEM APART?
  ISBN 978-1-4342-3278-6 (LIBRARY BINDING)
  1. DATING (SOCIAL CUSTOMS)--JUVENILE FICTION. 2. HIGH
SCHOOLS--JUVENILE FICTION. 3. BEST FRIENDS--JUVENILE FICTION.
4. FRIENDSHIP--JUVENILE FICTION. 5. TRUST--JUVENILE FICTION. [1.
DATING (SOCIAL CUSTOMS)--FICTION. 2. HIGH SCHOOLS--FICTION.
3. SCHOOLS--FICTION. 4. BEST FRIENDS--FICTION. 5. FRIENDSHIP--
FICTION. 6. TRUST--FICTION.] I. TITLE.
  PZ7.G13543TE 2012
  813.6--DC23

                                    2011040747

GRAPHIC DESIGNER: KAY FRASER
PRODUCTION SPECIALIST: MICHELLE BIEDSCHEID
ART CREDITS FOR COVER AND INTERIORS: SHUTTERSTOCK

PRINTED IN THE UNITED STATES OF AMERICA IN BRAINERD,
MINNESOTA.
102011   006406BANGS12

CLAUDIA & *Monica*: FRESHMAN GIRLS

We've been friends forever.
And now we're in high school.
Two best friends,
getting ready to face
the world of boys,
homework, tests, romance,
and growing up.

Thank goodness we have each other.

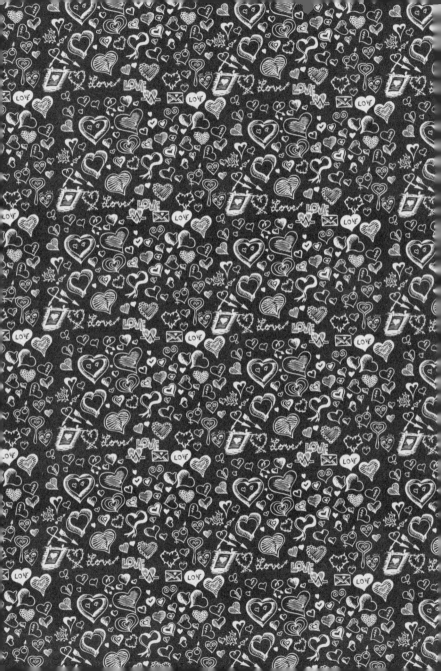

CHAPTER 1

The last time I saw Eric Weaver, we were nine. Let's just say that visit wasn't the start of a beautiful friendship.

My mom and Vivian, Eric's mom, have been best friends since college. The Weavers live in another state, so Viv and my mom don't see each other very often, but they email and call all the time.

It's been six years since Mom and I went to visit Eric and his mom at their house in Virginia.

Eric was the meanest, most annoying boy I'd ever met. Ever. He put a plastic snake in my bed. He glued the bristles of my toothbrush together. He dumped a bowl of cereal in my lap. I was terrified of mice, and he told me there were mice in the room I was sleeping in at his house. I couldn't wait to go home.

I'm still scarred for life.

But it's been six years. I've changed a lot in six years, and I hope Eric has, too. I mean, we were little kids. I was still wearing Princess Patsy jammies when I was nine. Eric had really big teeth and scabby knees and skinny legs.

Now I'm fifteen and I have a boyfriend and I'm in high school. Eric's fifteen too. Maybe he has a girlfriend. Maybe he's grown up a little.

A girl can dream, right?

Well, even if he hasn't grown up to be cool and nice, I'm sure I can handle whatever the weekend brings.

Right?

Right?

Ugh.

* * *

As soon as we show up on Viv's doorstep, I start to feel better. Viv is really cool, more like a big sister than my mom's friend. She has always treated me like an adult. She sends me great presents on my birthday—last year it was an amazing scarf that brings out the honey tones in my eyes—and I totally trust her with secrets.

She's the best. And she welcomes me with a huge hug the minute she opens the door.

"I can't believe it!" she says. "You look grown-up in your FriendBook photos, but in real life? You're amazing!"

I laugh. "Thanks," I say.

Then she steps aside to hug my mom, and while they're shrieking and cooing over each other, I glance through the open door and gasp.

One of the hottest guys I've ever seen in my life is standing there. He's not as cute as Rory, but he's muscular and tall and strong. "Eric?" I say.

"Monica?" he says. "Whoa. You look—you look really different."

I laugh. "Um, thanks?" I say. "I think."

"Yeah," he says. "You look great."

"You do too," I say, smiling.

"When did you get so pretty?" he asks.

"When did you get tall?" I counter.

"Last week," he jokes, grinning. "Just happened all of a sudden. It was kind of embarrassing, because I was in public at the time, but—"

"Oh, quit your flirting and give me a hug," my mom tells him. "Monica has a boyfriend."

I feel my face getting hot, and a definite look of disappointment crosses Eric's face. "For real?" he says. When I nod, he winks and adds, "Maybe you HAD a boyfriend."

"No," I say. "I'm pretty sure I do, and will continue to, have a boyfriend."

"I just baked blueberry muffins," Viv says, changing the subject.

"I love blueberry muffins!" I exclaim. "And yours are the best."

"I know," Viv says, smiling. "That's why I made them."

Mom goes into the kitchen with Viv. Right away, they start gossiping about people they went to school with.

Eric helps me carry our bags into the guest room. In fact, he's super sweet, a huge change from six years ago. He doesn't insult me or try to trip me or brush off imaginary germs when I walk by him. He opens doors instead! Weird.

"Forget the stupid muffins," he says once we're alone. "Let's go get pizza at Papa Pete's." Eric puts his arm around my shoulders. "My friends hang out there on Fridays, and I can't wait to introduce you to them. You'll love them. It's a really great group."

I'm so flustered that I freeze. I can't tell if Eric is flirting or just being nice. It feels like flirting, but he knows I have a boyfriend. Either way, I don't want to be hugged.

I twist out from under his arm and smile. "That sounds really fun, but I love blueberry muffins," I say. "And I remember your mom's being the best. Plus, I had pizza last night!"

"Your loss," Eric says, shrugging. Then he winks at me. "You'll wish you changed your mind."

Does he mean about pizza or him? I wonder as I dash into the kitchen.

* * *

After we eat, Mom and Viv stay in the kitchen to talk. Right away, it's pretty clear that Eric is bored by their conversation.

"I just got a bunch of new movies," he says. "You want to watch one?"

"Uh, sure," I say. "Let me just call my boyfriend first to say goodnight."

"Okay," he says. "Meet me in the living room when you're done."

I step outside to call Rory, but he doesn't answer. I sigh. I really wanted to talk to him. This is the first time I've been away on a weekend since we started dating. It's strange to spend a Friday evening with some other guy! But I know Rory works a lot of Fridays, and he mentioned he was going to work this weekend. So that's probably where he is.

Eric and I watch monster movies in the living room. He scoots too close on the sofa and drapes his arm across the top. When he touches my shoulder and tries to pull me closer, I jump up.

"I have a boyfriend," I say. "Remember? I mentioned him before."

Eric shrugs. "He's not here. And anyway, I'm just being friendly."

I pretend to check my watch. "Whoa, it's late," I say. "And I'm exhausted from the drive. I think I'm going to go to bed."

Eric frowns. "Aw, sleep well," he says. "See you tomorrow."

I read in bed till my mom comes into the room. "How is it seeing Viv?" I ask while she pulls on her pajamas.

"Oh, it's great," she says. "And we are both so thrilled that you and Eric are getting along! What a change from last time we visited."

I laugh nervously. "Yeah," I say. "He's great."

Mom yawns. "I'm going to hit the hay," she says. "We have a full day of shopping ahead of us!"

"Okay," I say. "Sleep tight. I'm just going to finish this chapter."

Mom smiles at me. "I'm so glad you came with me, honey. I know Eric wasn't your favorite person last time we visited, and it just means so much to me that you two are trying again."

* * *

Eric is waiting in the kitchen the next morning. "I have *Four Kingdoms* loaded and ready to go in the

TV room," he says. "Do you know it? It's a great game. You'll love it, I promise."

"You've got time," Mom says, smiling over at me from across the table. "We aren't going to the mall for a couple of hours."

"I have homework," I say. "I should finish that before we hit the stores." I lock the guest room door and send Claudia a text.

Help!

Claudia answers right away. *What's the matter?*

Eric! I type.

Is he still a brat?

He's being nice.

Is that bad? she asks.

I want to explain how his being nice feels a little more like him being flirty, but I change my mind.

No, just weird. :) I guess we're going to the mall soon. XOXO

Have fun shopping!

Luckily, I talk Mom and Viv into leaving for the mall sooner than they planned. And once we're safely out of the house, I start really having fun. I love hanging out with Mom and Viv.

We have brunch at Gabby's Grill, and I have the best eggs Benedict of all time. After that, I buy a new outfit. Mom and Vivian try on dozens of shoes at several stores, but they don't buy any. We stop for coffee about halfway through, and then spend the afternoon window shopping in the really expensive stores.

By the time we get back to Viv's, I'm starving and exhausted. "What's for dinner?" I ask when we park in Viv and Eric's driveway. "Shopping makes me hungry."

"It mostly just makes me tired," my mom admits.

"Worth it," Viv says.

"Totally worth it!" I say. "A day of great food, shopping, and being fabulous? You can't beat that!"

Viv laughs. "You've got a little fashionista on your hands," she says to my mom.

My mom rolls her eyes. "No kidding," she says. "Ever since she started high school."

We carry in the bags and collapse on the couches in the living room.

"So, dinner plans?" I ask.

"Your mom and I are going out to dinner with some other friends from school," Viv says. "We can drop you and Eric off at the mall on our way to the restaurant."

"Oh!" I say, trying to be cool. "Okay."

"Sounds good, right?" Eric says, walking in.

"You can see a movie and get something to eat at the food court," Mom adds.

I don't want to be a problem. Mom hardly ever gets a weekend off from her uber-busy job, and she's been really looking forward to seeing her old friends for, like, weeks. But I do not want to go anywhere alone with Eric!

"Some of my friends will be there," Eric says. "We all want to see *Mars at Midnight.*"

"Oh!" I say. "That sounds okay, I guess." That makes me feel better. Going out in a group will be fun, and it won't seem like a date. Plus, I'm working on being braver about hanging out with people I don't know. This is great practice.

I try calling Rory again, but he doesn't answer. So I just send a text.

Miss you.

After a few minutes, he writes back.

Miss you too. I'm working double shifts all weekend to keep my mind off you.

Obviously, I melt.

· MONICA ·

CHAPTER 2

CLAUDIA

I hate it when Monica's out of town.

It's not like I can't do things on my own. It's just more fun to do things with my best friend.

We spend most weekends together, hanging out. We love going to the mall, seeing movies, going out to eat, just grabbing coffee at Casey's . . . whatever we want.

And now that we have boyfriends, it's even more fun to hang out as a group. The four of us go on a double date almost every weekend. In fact, we go out together more than Brad and I go out alone.

But this weekend, Monica is visiting her mom's friend. She's two states away, shopping and relaxing. And I'm in misery!

Not really, of course. Actually, Monica's probably having a worse time than I am. Last time she visited these people, her mom's friend's kid was absolutely horrible to her.

Monica's kind of sensitive, and she could not take his teasing and bullying. I tried to tell her it seemed like the guy was flirting, in his weird nine-year-old way, but she wouldn't listen. She was totally traumatized by the whole thing.

Her mom basically guilt-tripped her into going on this trip by saying Mon was growing up so fast, they never spent any time together since she and Rory started dating, blah blah blah. And of course it worked.

Well, that and the promise of going to a great mall and hanging out with Viv, who sounds really cool. And it sounds like Eric's being really nice, according to Monica's texts. She sounds a little frantic in them, but that's Monica. Like I said, she's kind of sensitive.

Anyway, since Monica is out of town, by Saturday afternoon I'm bored and looking for plans. I send Brad a couple of texts, but when I don't hear back, I figure he's busy and that I'm stuck at home with my mom and dad for the night.

Luckily, before the situation gets too frightening, Brad calls.

"Hello, you," I say. "What's going on?"

Brad says, "Oh, not much. Sorry I didn't get back to your texts earlier. My mom dragged me out doing errands with her, and then my dad got me to help him with the garage."

"Was that fun?" I ask.

Brad snorts. "Not really," he says. "He drilled me a lot about you and me. Actually, my mom did too." He sighs. "I kind of feel like she was trying to get information, and when she didn't get the answers she wanted, she got my dad to ask more questions."

"What did they ask?" I say, feeling my face heat up. Parents can be so embarrassing.

"Oh, you know," Brad says. "Usual parent stuff. I mean, haven't your parents been giving you the third degree ever since we started dating? Mine have been super weird."

I think. "I guess so," I say. My dad has been texting me a lot more often, and my mom always wants to know exactly where I'm going to be. "But I sort of figured they've just been extra clingy because I'm in high school now."

Brad is quiet for a second. "They know we're dating, right?" he asks.

I laugh. "Of course they do," I say. "You're like, all I talk about."

"Well, that explains it," Brad says. "If you talk about me all the time, they get enough information. Then they don't have to ask questions."

"I guess," I say. "Don't you talk about me to your parents?"

"Not really," he says.

It's weird. I know it shouldn't bother me. Boys don't talk to their parents as much as girls do sometimes, and I'm pretty open with my mom and dad. But it hurts my feelings that Brad doesn't talk about me at home.

Then he adds, "I kind of just want to keep you to myself, you know? Once they start asking questions, it feels like they're prying into our private relationship."

I smile. "I know what you mean," I admit quietly. "It's not like I tell my mom and dad about kissing you."

He laughs. "I hope not," he says. "That would be kind of awkward."

"No kidding!" I say.

Brad changes the subject. "What are you and Monica up to tonight?" he asks.

I sigh. "She's out of town this weekend, remember?"

"Oh, right," he says. "Visiting her mom's friend and that weird guy. I forgot."

"Yeah," I say. "I got a couple of texts from her earlier. Sounds like she's having an okay time."

Brad says, "That's good. Does that mean you're free tonight?"

I pretend to check a calendar. "Well, I'd have to move a few things around . . ."

"Really?" he asks, sounding disappointed.

I laugh. "No, silly," I say. "I'm free. You want to do something?"

"Definitely," Brad says. "Pizza? Just me and you?"

"That sounds incredible," I say. "Can't wait."

· CLAUDIA ·

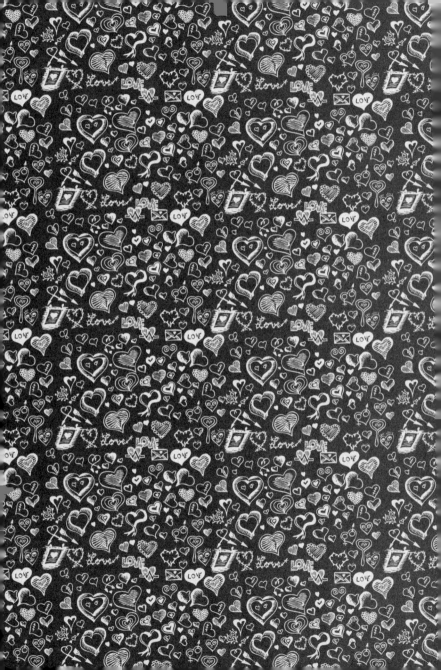

"You look great," Eric says as we get into the car. I don't care about impressing anyone, but I changed into my favorite jeans and a cute sweater, and pulled on a pair of adorable heels.

"Thanks." I smile.

Eric looks good, too, but I don't return the compliment. In fact, I feel guilty for noticing! Shouldn't I only notice when Rory looks good?

Viv drops us off at the main entrance into the mall. "We'll pick you up here between 9:45 and 10," she says.

"We'll be at Ronny's Steak House!" Mom calls out as they pull away.

Eric checks his watch. "We'd better hurry. I hate walking into movies late."

"I do too," I say.

We get in line. When we reach the front, I open my mouth to tell the ticket girl what movie I want, but Eric cuts me off.

"We'll take two for the 7:05 *Mars at Midnight*," he says.

I grab some money from my purse, but he quickly gives her the money. "It's on me," he says, smiling.

"Thanks," I say, smiling back. "That's really nice of you."

"No problem," he tells me. "I don't get to pay for a pretty girl to see a movie that often." Then he winks.

I'm hoping he's still just being friendly. "Where are your friends?" I ask.

"They're probably inside," he says.

"What if they're just late?" I ask. My friends wouldn't go in before everyone arrived. They'd wait for everyone to get there.

"Then they'll miss the beginning. Come on, it doesn't matter." Eric hands in our tickets and we walk into the dimly lit theater. He doesn't look for his friends. He just heads for an empty row of seats in the middle. "Is this okay?" he asks.

"What about your friends?" I ask. "Did you look for them?"

He looks down, and that's when I know. Eric's friends aren't coming. In fact, I doubt Eric's friends were ever coming.

I look him in the eye. "You lied to me about meeting friends, didn't you," I say, crossing my arms. "Why would you do that?"

"Guilty as charged," Eric says. "I knew if you didn't come, my mom would make me stay home, too. That just seemed dumb. I really want to see this movie."

I sigh. "Okay," I say. "Whatever. I just think you could have explained that instead of lying about it."

"I know. I'm really sorry, Monica," he says. "How about I make it up to you? Popcorn?"

"With butter," I say. As he turns to leave, I add, "And some Raisinettes."

Eric laughs. "You got it," he says.

The movie is great. I spend so much time laughing that I forget about being mad that Eric lied to me. Afterward, we're both in a great mood.

"What do you want to eat?" Eric asks as we head toward the food court.

"Tacos or Chinese," I say.

"We could do both," Eric says.

"Great idea!" I say. We high five.

The food isn't bad, and Eric keeps me laughing with hilarious stories about his school. I feel a little weird because I'm having fun with a boy who isn't Rory. Then I remind myself that Eric and I are just friends.

Even if I do think he's a little cute.

We arrive at our pick-up point at exactly 9:45. Eric checks outside, but his mom isn't waiting at the curb. We sit on a bench to wait.

"Did you have a good time tonight?" Eric asks.

"Yes, I did," I say. "This has been a really fun day."

"Good," Eric says.

Then he leans over and kisses me.

CHAPTER 4

CLAUDIA

Brad told me to meet him at Pizza Palace at 6:30, so I get Jimmy to drop me off there at 6:15. I like to be early.

Brad, on the other hand, isn't super punctual. He shows up about ten minutes late. I'm used to it.

"Sorry, sweetie," he says after kissing me hello. "My mom had to finish gardening or something, so we got a late start. Forgive me?"

I smile and nod. "Of course," I say. "Not a big deal."

"I can't wait till I get a car, like Rory," Brad says,

looking wistful. "It'll be so sweet to be able to pick you up and take you on dates and stuff."

I smile. "Yeah, it will be really nice," I say. "Plus, I won't have to take the bus anymore!"

"Bonus," Brad says, smiling back at me. "Let's sit down."

We get a table and order sodas. Then we look at the menu.

"Do you want to split a pizza?" Brad asks.

"Sure," I say. "Pepperoni and hot peppers?"

Brad makes a face. "How about sausage and extra cheese?" he asks.

We smile at each other. "Let's split it down the middle," I suggest. "Half your way and half mine."

"That sounds good," Brad says.

After the server takes our order, Brad and I are quiet for a few minutes. "So," I say finally. "What are you doing tomorrow?"

"Going to the game with my dad," he says. "What about you?"

I shrug. "Waiting around until Monica gets back, I guess," I say. "I haven't heard from her since this morning, so I don't know what time she's arriving home."

Then we're quiet for a little bit longer.

I start to get nervous. Why don't we have anything to say to each other? Is it okay if we're not spending the whole meal chatting like crazy about everything and anything?

"I'm glad you weren't busy tonight," Brad says. "I like going out with Rory and Monica, but it's really nice to have you all to myself."

That makes me relax. "Me too," I say. "I do like double dates, but this is great too."

"We should do this more," Brad says. "I mean, I know we go on dates together, but usually it's like, to a movie or something. We hardly ever just sit and talk. And I like talking to you so much. It's like, one of my favorite things to do."

I smile and feel my face heating up. "I like talking to you too," I say.

Brad reaches across the table and takes my hand. "I know I told you that I love you at the Halloween party," he says. "I hope you know that I really meant it. I wasn't just saying it because we were at the party."

I look down. "I know," I say. "I mean, I didn't think you were just saying it."

"Good," Brad says. "Because I definitely wasn't. I—"

Just then, the server brings our pizza over. It smells delicious. I start to take a piece, but Brad says, "Wait!"

"Why?" I ask, confused. "Is something wrong with it? Did they give us the wrong toppings?"

"No," Brad says. He smiles. "You can't bite pizza as soon as it's put on the table," he says. "I mean, come on! Look how hot it is!"

He's right. The cheese is practically still bubbling. "Thanks for the warning," I say. I put the pizza back down.

"I don't want you to burn your mouth," Brad adds. "I don't want it to hurt when I'm kissing you later."

My face feels like it's on fire. "Okay. Then I'll wait," I say.

"Anyway," Brad says, "I just wanted to make sure you knew that. About me saying I love you."

"I do," I say.

Brad looks like he's waiting for me to say something.

"What?" I ask finally.

"Do you . . ." He pauses, looking at me. It almost looks like he's blushing.

"Do I what?" I ask.

"Do you love me back?" he whispers.

"Brad!" I almost shout. "Of course! I said I did that night! I said it right after you told me!"

He raises his eyebrows. "Really?" he asks. He laughs. "Oh, my gosh. I'm really relieved. I guess I didn't hear you. Did you whisper it or something?"

"Yes, I think so," I say.

Really, I remember it vividly: how he hugged me, how his skin smelled. And yeah, I had whispered.

We both laugh. "Oh, man," Brad says. "I'm kind of embarrassed right now."

"Don't be," I say, reaching across to take his hand. "I like saying it. I love you."

"I love you, Claudia," he says.

And then we eat our pizza.

· CLAUDIA ·

CHAPTER 5

Monica

I can't look at Eric at breakfast on Sunday morning. In fact, I can barely even talk. I know Mom and Viv are exchanging looks over the table, but I don't care. I don't feel like talking.

Mom and Viv try to start conversations, and Eric talks and talks, but I just stare at my food. As soon as I'm done eating, I push my chair away, go to the guest room, and pack my things.

I hardly talk to Mom on the drive home, either. I just put my headphones in and listen to music for the whole six-hour drive. Rory texts me a few times, but I don't respond. I feel anxious every time my phone beeps.

"Did something go wrong?" Mom asks finally, when we're about an hour away from home.

"What do you mean?" I ask. I know what she means, obviously, but I don't really know how to answer her. So I'm stalling.

"Last night, you were in a great mood when we dropped you off," Mom says. "And when we picked you and Eric up, you weren't talking and you seemed upset. I should have asked you about it last night, but I was so tired. I'm sorry, honey."

I shake my head. "Nothing went wrong," I say. I don't like lying to my mom, but I also don't want to tell her what Eric did. She'd tell Viv, and I don't want to have to deal with that right now. I just want to forget the whole thing ever happened.

"Are you sure, Monica?" Mom asks.

"Yes," I say. I pick up my phone and pretend like I'm texting someone.

"Okay," Mom says softly. "I just hope you'll tell me eventually what's bugging you."

I sigh.

"Fine," I say finally. "Eric kissed me. That's what's wrong."

Mom's face turns angry. "Are you serious?" she says. "He kissed you? At the movies, or what?"

"Yes," I say. "Not at the movies. While we were waiting for you and Viv. And he lied about his friends meeting us."

She shakes her head. "You've got to be kidding me," she mutters. "I knew I shouldn't have let you go to that movie with him."

"I feel awful," I admit. Tears spring to my eyes.

"About Rory?" Mom asks. I nod, and she says, "Oh, honey. He will understand. He'll want to kill Eric, but he won't be mad at you. I promise. Rory's a good guy."

"Unlike Eric," I mutter.

CHAPTER 6

CLAUDIA

I've always liked school. I'm not a huge fan of homework, but I'm super curious and interested in everything — except maybe chemistry. Not the romantic kind like I have with Brad, but the mixing stuff together to see what happens kind that can stink up a classroom. That might be the one school activity I just don't care for one bit.

So anyway, I like being at school. And I'm anxious to get to homeroom this morning. I haven't heard from Monica since her text on Saturday. And I only saw Brad for our pizza date.

As usual, he saves me a seat.

"Did you get your homework done?" I ask.

"Enough to stay out of trouble," Brad jokes. He's smart, but he spends more time on sports than studying.

Just then, Monica rushes in and sits in the seat I saved for her.

"Yay!" I say. "You're here! How was your trip?"

"Fine," Monica says. She doesn't say anything else, and then class starts and we can't talk anymore.

We can't talk before second period, either. "I'll see you at lunch!" I tell Monica as Anna and I head down the hall.

"Later!" Monica waves. She smiles, but it's a weird smile.

Something's up with her.

* * *

Monica and Rory are already eating when Brad and I sit down.

"How was your trip? Did you have fun shopping with your mom?" I ask.

Monica nods and takes another bite of her sandwich.

"Did you buy anything?" I ask.

Monica swallows. "Jeans and a top."

But she's wearing clothes I've seen before. I wonder why she didn't wear her new things. I always do the first chance I get.

"What else did you do?" I press.

"Mom and Viv talked," Monica says crisply. "I watched TV and read a book." She doesn't look at me or Rory. She exhales like she's super annoyed and attacks her sandwich.

I frown. Something is seriously wrong. Is Monica mad at Rory? Is he mad at her?

Rory turns to Brad. "Did you talk to Ms. Feeny?"

Brad shakes his head. "I'm not that brave," he says.

"She's pretty scary," Rory says. "But if you don't get a good grade on the English midterm, Coach has to kick you off the basketball team."

"What? Brad, you didn't tell me that," I say, looking at him.

Brad blushes. "I know. I was embarrassed, I guess," he says.

"Do you want to study together tonight at my house?" I ask.

He smiles and puts his arm around me. "Do we have to actually study?" he asks, winking.

I shrug his arm away. "Uh, yeah," I say. "Especially if it means you'll be able to stay on the basketball team."

"Okay, okay," he says. "Studying it is." He puts his arm around me again and squeezes my shoulders. I can't help grinning.

"Well, maybe we don't have to spend the whole time studying," I say, resting my head on his shoulder.

"Gross," Tommy says, sitting down next to me. Then he changes the subject to basketball practice. He's the announcer for the games, so he wants to go to practice to work on material.

"You don't need material for games," Rory says, rolling his eyes. "You just announce the players."

"I know," Tommy says with his mouth full. He swallows and adds, "But I want to make the announcements a little more interesting, you know?"

"Oh, no," Brad groans. "Telling Coach to pick you for announcer is going to come back to haunt me, isn't it."

We all laugh. But when I try to catch Monica's eye, she just looks down.

Something is definitely up.

When the bell rings, Rory and Monica walk out of the cafeteria with us.

Brad says, "So we'll study tonight, right?"

"Definitely," I say. "You'll get an A on your test."

"You know anything about geometry?" Rory

asks. He and Monica are holding hands, but she still looks upset. Or weird. Or something.

"Sorry," I say. "But Monica's good at math."

"Oh. Right," she says. "I could maybe help you out. But not tonight," she says in a rush.

Rory frowns, but then he shrugs. "No big deal. I have to work tonight anyway."

We're walking past the bathroom when Monica says, "I feel sick. See you guys later." She ducks inside the door.

Rory looks worried. "Will you make sure she's okay, Claud?" he asks.

"Of course," I say. I give Brad a quick kiss. "See you two in study hall."

Inside the restroom, Monica's leaning on a sink. It looks like she's trying not to cry—or throw up— or both.

"What's wrong?" I put my hand on her back. "Did you catch the flu or something?"

Monica shakes her head. "Worse."

"What could be worse than the flu?"

Monica quickly scans the stall doors to make sure we're alone. "You have to swear you won't say a word about this to anyone. Not even your cat."

I hold up my right hand. "I swear."

Monica sighs. Then she blurts out, "I kissed someone else."

CHAPTER 7

Monica

"You what?" Claudia stares at me in shock.

"Eric kissed me," I say. "I didn't kiss him back."

Claudia gasps. "Are you serious?"

I nod. I'm so upset that I'm shaking. "It happened so fast." Tears start to stream from my eyes. I know we're late for class, but I don't even care.

Claudia hands me a paper towel. "Here. Calm down and start at the beginning."

"Okay." I dab my eyes and take a deep breath. "So, right when we got there, Eric was super flirty. He kept putting his arm around me. I told him I had a boyfriend, and he was like, 'Yeah, but he's not here.' Then he tricked me into basically going on a date with him."

"How?" Claudia asks.

"Mom and Viv had dinner plans," I explain. "I didn't want them to feel bad about leaving me alone, and Eric said his friends would be at the movie."

"So what went wrong?" Claudia asks.

"The friends were not at the movie," I say.

"So he lied?" Claudia crosses her arms angrily. I can't help but smile.

"Yeah," I say. "He even admitted it! I couldn't leave so we watched the movie and got something to eat. It was actually really fun, and he wasn't trying to hold my hand or anything. We were just acting like friends. Or so I thought, until we were waiting for our ride. Then he just suddenly kissed me. On the lips!"

"What a jerk!" Claudia exclaims.

"Totally," I say. "He didn't apologize or anything. He thought it was funny. I feel like he thought he'd just give it a shot and maybe I'd choose him over Rory."

"It's not funny," Claudia says, frowning. "And obviously you'd never pick some loser like him over an awesome guy like Rory."

"Of course not," I say. "But now I feel terrible. I know I should tell Rory, but I know it'll really make him mad."

"It wasn't your fault," Claudia says.

"I know, but I still feel guilty." I sigh.

"Maybe you shouldn't tell Rory," she says.

"I don't want him to hear about it from someone else."

"Who's going to tell him?" Claudia asks. "Nobody knows but me and Eric, and I promised not to tell anyone."

"That's true," I say.

"You didn't do anything wrong, so why

confess?" Claudia asks. "What if Rory thinks there's more to it?"

I nod. That's a good point.

"Look," she says firmly. "You feel guilty so you'll act guilty. That's just how you are, Monica. You don't hide your feelings very well."

Keeping a secret from Rory—especially about a stolen kiss—doesn't feel right. But Claudia has a point.

"Thanks for the advice, Claudia," I say. "I'll think about it."

* * *

I don't see Rory until 7th period study hall. He's sitting with Claudia and Brad when I walk in. I join them and try to act like nothing's wrong.

Rory gives me a quick kiss. Then he turns back to his math homework.

"Hi, Monica," Brad says. "How's it going?"

"Fine," I say a little too quickly. "Everything's great. Nothing new is happening with me. I'm just doing what I always do—"

Claudia kicks me under the table, and I feel my face heat up. I'm babbling like someone who has something to hide.

I shut up. Rory doesn't notice anyway. He's totally focused on a math problem. "I don't get this," Rory says.

"What?" Brad asks. "Maybe I can help."

Rory frowns. "Do you know anything about angle supplements and complements?"

"Nope," Brad says.

Claudia shrugs and shakes her head. "Me either," she says.

I'm good at math, but I'm taking ninth grade algebra. "That's beyond what I know," I admit. "Sorry."

Rory glances at a table of other sophomores. "Maybe someone over there can help."

"Go ask," I say. "I can survive one study hall without you."

Rory pretends to be hurt. "You can?"

"Not really," I say, "but I don't want you to flunk geometry."

Rory grins and starts stacking up his books and notebooks. "Are you busy after school? I have to find a present for my grandma, and I could really use your help."

"Sounds great," I say.

✳ ✳ ✳

Rory meets me at my locker right away after school. "Ready?" he asks, leaning over to kiss me.

I pull away from the kiss and say, "Definitely."

I still feel guilty about the Eric kiss and keeping it a secret. I think I should tell him, but I haven't absolutely decided to do it yet. I'm a bundle of nerves, but Rory doesn't notice. His mind is on geometry. "I've never been good at math," he says, "but I've never had this much trouble."

"Did anyone else know what was going on?" I ask.

"Yeah, but that didn't really help," Rory says. "When they tried to explain it, I just got more confused."

We slide into his beat-up old car. "What are you going to do?" I ask as he drives out of the parking lot.

"I'll think of something," he says, "but I don't want to think about it now. Let's just go to the mall and have fun."

I reach over and pretend to check if he has a fever. "Are you okay?" I ask, smiling. "You hate shopping!"

He gazes into my eyes. "Monica, I don't hate anything I do with you," he says. Then he reaches over and takes my hand. I feel my insides get all warm and mushy.

"You're so sweet," I murmur. But as soon as I say it, I feel guilty again. I take my hand away and change the subject back to basketball.

Once we're inside the mall, I start to feel a little better.

I love the Towne Mall. It looks like a future city with potted trees and flowers, a big center dome, and a hundred stores. The food court has burgers, subs, sushi, and tacos, and the movie theater has like fourteen screens.

Mostly I just like walking around looking at stuff, especially when Rory and I are holding hands. I feel normal again when we're there.

"What do you want to get your grandma?" I ask.

"I don't know," Rory says. "That's why you're here."

I fake a frown. "Is that the only reason?"

Rory pretends to think about it. "No, I guess not." He grins and squeezes my hand.

We head for Parkers, the most expensive (and

best) department store. "When I'm stumped about a present, I walk up and down the aisles here," I tell him. "I usually know the perfect gift when I see it."

"Okay," Rory says, but he doesn't sound convinced.

We walk past racks of beautiful clothes and shoes, but Rory isn't interested. He doesn't know his grandma's size, and he doesn't want to get something she might have to return.

I find several pairs of pretty earrings. "I love these, and they're not too expensive," I say.

Rory holds up the dangly silver earrings. "She never wears earrings that look like chandeliers."

I laugh. "Okay," I say. "Let's check the home department."

I point out a bunch of unusual kitchen gadgets and some adorable guest towels.

"No," Rory says. "I want something practical and personal. Something she'll use all the time."

I'm getting a little frustrated. I'm sure Rory's

grandma will love whatever he gets her. Grandmas are like that. But it's his present.

Rory stops suddenly. "Do you see something?" I ask.

"No, I smell it," he says. "Hold on."

Rory steps up to the perfume counter. "What scent is that?" he asks the sales clerk.

"It's called Morning Mist," the woman says.

"My grandma loves that stuff," Rory tells me. "She wears it every day."

"Then that's what you should get her," I say.

Rory frowns when he checks the price. "If I buy this, I won't have enough left for something at the food court."

"No problem," I say. "I'm buying today."

After we leave the store, we head to Taco Joe's.

"Do you have wrapping paper and a card?" I ask.

Rory smacks his forehead. "No! I didn't even think of it."

"No worries," I say. "We can stop at the gift shop on the way out."

Rory slips his arm over the back of my chair and looks into my eyes. "What would I do without you?"

I just shrug and smile.

But my good mood slips away. He doesn't know that someone else kissed me.

I can't tell him. But can I keep it inside forever?

CHAPTER 8

CLAUDIA

I can't concentrate on my homework. I don't know if I gave Monica the right advice. I mean, if Brad told me that some girl kissed him, I'd be really upset. And I think I'd want to know. I'd rather know than not know.

Wouldn't I?

And it would bring up so many questions. Like: Did Brad flirt with her? On purpose or was he just being nice? Did he pull away instantly? Or did the surprise kiss linger?

Kisses don't just happen, do they?

Of course, I know how girls think. Maybe boys aren't as suspicious.

I have to find out or I won't be able to sleep, so I call Brad.

"I was just thinking about you," Brad says.

I smile. "I need a guy's opinion about something," I tell him.

"I am a guy. What can I tell you?" Brad asks.

"First you have to swear that you won't tell anyone what I'm going to tell you." I totally trust Brad. He never goes back on his word.

"I promise," Brad says. "Your secret is safe with me."

"It's not my secret," I say. "It's Monica's."

"Okay," Brad says.

"So, you know how she was visiting her mom's friend last weekend?"

"Yeah," he says. "Shopping, or something."

"Right," I say. "Well, her mom's friend has a kid

our age named Eric. And apparently he tricked her into going on a date with him, and then he kissed her."

Brad is quiet for a second. "How did he trick her into going on a date?" he asks. "I mean, if she went, it kind of sounds like she wanted to go."

"She wanted to see the movie, and the guy said his friends were going too," I explain. "She definitely didn't want it to be a date."

"Maybe Rory and I should pay Eric a surprise visit," Brad says. He sounds as angry as I feel.

"You can't. He lives in another state," I say. "And Rory doesn't know."

"What? Why didn't Monica tell him?" Brad asks.

"Why should she? She didn't do anything wrong."

"But she's Rory's girlfriend," Brad argues. "She should tell him everything."

"What if he blames her?" I ask.

"He won't," Brad says. "Trust me."

I want to call Monica as soon as Brad hangs up, but it's too late. I decide that I'll talk to her first thing in the morning, as soon as we get to school. I'll find a way to get some private time with her.

I read a few chapters of my book before I get ready for bed. Then, just as I'm about to turn off the light, I get a text.

Monica made out with another guy! She cheated on Rory!

I get the same text again and again, from a bunch of different people.

My heart is pounding. The juicy rumor is flying around school, but I don't know how it got started.

Needless to say, I hardly sleep.

* * *

The next morning, I feel like a zombie. Gina Tanner sees me get off the bus. "Can you believe it?" she says, running up to me. "How could Monica cheat on Rory like that?"

"She didn't," I say. "You can't believe everything you hear."

Gina raises her eyebrow. "Yeah right," she says. "Gossip doesn't start without a reason. It's true."

Twisted truth, I think, but there's no point explaining that to Gina. She likes Rory, so she hates Monica.

"I would never cheat on Rory," Gina says.

You'll never get a chance, I think. Rory can't stand Gina. "Who told you?" I ask.

"All the cheerleaders and a dozen other people," Gina says.

I desperately want to know who started the rumor. I don't want Monica to blame me.

I brace myself when I see Monica outside homeroom. She walks in with me. "Did Mrs. Marino hint about a science quiz in your class yesterday?" Monica asks.

"Uh, no, I—" I stammer. "I don't think so."

Anna and Carly are whispering together. They stop and look up when Monica and I sit down. Monica doesn't seem to notice.

"I'm not ready for a test," Monica goes on. "And I feel like she said something that made me think there might be one."

Tommy and Chloe walk in. When Tommy sees Monica, he whispers in Chloe's ear.

"What?" Chloe gasps and slaps a hand over her mouth.

Monica glances at Chloe, but she doesn't look upset.

I'm astounded. Everyone has heard the terrible, untrue gossip about Monica—except Monica.

The subject of a horrible rumor is always the last to hear it. But sooner or later, Monica will hear it. Then she'll be upset and furious at me.

I swore not to tell anyone that Eric kissed her.

But I did tell someone.

I told Brad.

And that has to mean Brad told someone.

* * *

Brad and I don't have the same second period class. I catch him before 3rd period web design gets started. "We need to talk," I say.

"I know," Brad says. He smiles and sits down. "Midterms are next week, and I still can't write a good essay."

"That's not what I want to talk about."

He can tell I'm mad. "Whoa," he says. "What's going on?"

I pause, breathe, and then blurt out my question. "Who did you tell about Monica's secret?"

"I didn't tell anyone." Brad says.

"There's a rumor going around that Monica cheated on Rory," I explain.

"I heard, but I didn't start it," Brad says. "I told you I wouldn't tell."

"But you're the only person I told," I say.

"Maybe Monica told someone else," Brad says.

"No way," I say. I'm positive about that. Monica told me because I'm her best friend, and she thought I'd keep my promise and my mouth shut. Just like I thought Brad would keep his word. That was a mistake.

"I didn't say a word," Brad says tightly. "I can't believe you'd think I would."

I stare at him, furious and hurt. He broke his promise, and now he's lying about it! I'm so upset I grab my backpack and change seats. When I look over at him, he's looking away. But his ears are red.

I can't believe how quickly my wonderful life fell apart.

I betrayed my best friend because I trusted a boy.

Then Brad betrayed me.

Great.

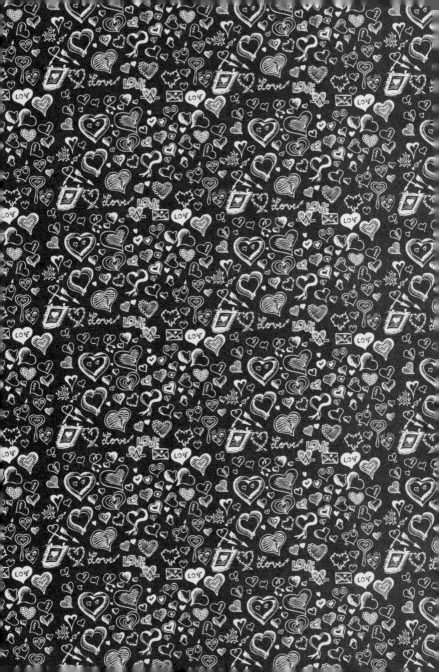

CHAPTER 9

Monica

Claudia dashes off after American History, just like she does every morning. She has 2nd period science in room 127. I have English on the second floor.

But walking through the halls is weird today. I feel like everyone is watching me and whispering behind my back. I just don't know why!

I duck into the nearest bathroom. Two sophomores are fixing their makeup by the sinks.

"She must be crazy!" the first girl exclaims.

"Unless the other guy is like, super cute or something," the second girl says.

When they see me, they stop talking and glance at each other. "Come on," the first girl says. "We're going to be late."

I look down at myself. My clothes look normal. My skirt isn't tucked into my underwear or anything. There's nothing on my face. I decide I must be imagining things. Then I make a mad dash down the hall.

I'm almost late for English. Chloe didn't save me a seat today. She's so busy talking to Tommy and Carly that she doesn't even see me come in.

There's an empty chair by Austin. He talks too much, but I don't have a choice. I sit down.

"Hi, Austin," I say. "How's it going?"

"Fine," Austin says. He doesn't talk about the latest DVD he bought or brag about his video game scores. He turns back to the book he's reading.

That's strange, I think. Austin never shuts up. That's why nobody wants to sit by him in English. Ms. Feeny loves to give detention for talking.

The bell rings so I can't ask Austin what's bothering him. I can't text Claudia to find out if she knows what's going on. Ms. Feeny loves to collect student cell phones, too.

Nothing odd happens in 3rd period Spanish. None of my friends are in that class. But as I'm walking to lunch, Sylvia catches me on the way to the cafeteria.

"Did you see this?" she asks. She holds out her cell phone, and I read the text. It's from a girl I don't know.

Monica Murray made out with another guy! She cheated on Rory!

I gasp, blink, and read it again. I don't want to believe my eyes, but the words are clear.

"Is it true?" Sylvia asks.

"No!" I exclaim. "Who sent this to you?"

"Everybody," Sylvia says. Then she recites a list. "Anna, Carly, Marco, Travis, Jenny, Tyler, Adam, Karen—"

I cut her off. "Thanks, Sylvia. I have to go."

I can't face anyone right now. I need time to think. I skip lunch and go to the library instead. My head spins as I try to sort out my thoughts.

Did Rory hear the rumor, too? He probably did. According to Sylvia, everybody has.

Will Rory understand when I explain?

How did people find out about Eric? Nobody has all the facts—except Claudia.

She swore not to tell anyone, but she obviously broke her promise. She knows I tried to push Eric away, so I know she didn't start the rumor. The person she told did. Claudia's betrayal hurts, but not as much as knowing that Rory might think I betrayed him.

I have to talk to him.

As soon as the bell rings, signaling the end of lunch, I head to Rory's math classroom. I see him just as I reach the classroom door. "Rory!" I call, rushing up to him. "I really need to talk to you."

Rory gives me a look. It's not a loving look or even a caring look. "I can't talk right now, Monica," he says, walking past me.

He goes into the classroom and sits down just as the bell rings.

Gina Tanner sits down next to him, and they start talking and laughing.

I feel terrible. Only one thing has changed since Rory and I had so much fun at the mall yesterday. Someone started a rumor that I cheated on him. And he thinks it's true because I took Claudia's advice and didn't tell him what really happened.

I don't want to talk to Claudia until I can get her alone.

* * *

Claudia and Brad are sitting at our usual study hall table when I walk in. They're not talking, and it looks kind of uncomfortable at their table.

Claudia looks up when I pause inside the door. She quickly looks away—probably because she feels guilty about what happened.

Good. I hope she feels guilty about it for the rest of her life! But even if she does, she'll never feel as guilty as I do.

I don't sit where we usually sit. Instead, I sit with Sylvia. We work on math together. She doesn't mention the whole cheating thing again. I'm grateful for that, at least. I know she wants to ask about it, but she doesn't.

I finish my homework just as the last bell rings. This time I rush out. I ambush Claudia at her locker. I'm furious, but I play calm. "Everyone in the whole school thinks I cheated on Rory," I say.

Claudia closes her eyes. "I know," she says.

"You're the only person I told about what happened with Eric," I say.

"Are you absolutely sure of that?" Claudia asks, frowning. "Couldn't you have told someone else?"

"I'm positive," I say. "There's no one else I would have told. I was upset, and I needed someone to talk to. You're the one person in the whole world I thought I could trust."

"I know how you feel," Claudia says quietly.

"This isn't about you, Claudia," I say angrily. "This is about me."

"I know, Monica," she says. Then she quickly adds, "But I wasn't sure if I gave you the right advice—about keeping the kiss a secret from Rory. So I asked Brad."

I gasp. "You told Brad?" I can't believe it. Seriously? After I asked her to keep it to herself?

"I didn't think he'd tell anyone!" Claudia looks really upset. "He promised."

I roll my eyes. "That's ridiculous!" I exclaim. "Brad and Rory are friends. He had to tell Rory someone else kissed me!"

CHAPTER 10

CLAUDIA

I sit by myself on the bus ride home. I don't feel like talking to anyone.

As soon as I get home, I call Monica, but she won't pick up. She won't even respond to my texts.

I feel terrible. Okay, so I didn't think Brad would tell anybody, but it's still no excuse. I swore I wouldn't tell anyone. That did not mean anyone but Brad.

I don't blame Monica for ignoring me. She thought she could trust me. I let her down because I trusted Brad. So now Monica's reputation is ruined and things are totally messed up between her and Rory. And there's nothing I can do about it.

I go to bed early, but I toss and turn all night. The next morning on the bus, I have a great idea. Feeling terrible isn't getting me anywhere, but maybe getting the truth out will help. It's so obvious, I should have thought of it right away. I get out my phone and send a text to as many people as I can think of.

Monica did not cheat on Rory! Some idiot kissed her even though she told him she had a boyfriend.

I'm in a better mood when I get to my locker. Yesterday, the false rumor about Monica hit every cell phone in school before first period. My text should make the rounds by lunch.

But my mood sours again when I reach homeroom. Monica isn't there yet, and Brad is sitting with Tyler by the windows. That's as far away from our usual group—and me—as he can get.

Brad sees me come in, but he quickly looks away. I rush toward my other friends. I know they all got my text. I hope somebody sends it to Monica. Then she'll know I tried to fix things.

"What does this mean?" Carly asks, pointing to her phone. My text is on the display screen.

"She had to be nice to him," I say as I sit down. "Monica went with her mom to visit an old friend last weekend. The guy who kissed her is the friend's son. She told him she had a boyfriend."

"Didn't he believe her?" Carly asks.

"Maybe he didn't care," Anna says.

"She should have stayed away," Jenny says.

"She tried," I say. "But Eric lied about meeting friends at the movies, and her mom was out to dinner so she couldn't get a ride. She told him to watch it and he did until—bam! He kissed her. No warning or anything."

"I should have known Monica wouldn't cheat on Rory, but I believed the rumor," Anna says.

"We all did," Jenny says.

Carly squints, puzzled. "How did the rumor get started anyway?"

"That's my fault," I say. When everyone gasps, I quickly explain. "I didn't start it. I needed a boy's opinion, so yeah, I told Brad—after he swore he wouldn't tell anyone else. He obviously didn't keep that promise."

"You think Brad started the rumor?" Anna looks shocked. "I don't believe it. He's a great secret-keeper."

"I don't want to believe he started the rumor," I say, "because he's my boyfriend and I trusted him. But the evidence is pretty clear. Monica didn't tell anyone else, and I only told Brad. Who else could have told everyone?"

"It just doesn't make sense," Anna says. "I don't know. I think there's more to it than just blaming Brad right away."

"I want to believe you're right," I say sadly. "I really do."

"I'm going to look into it," Anna says.

Monica comes in just before the bell rings. I can't talk to her now, but I'm determined to make things right between us before the end of the day.

* * *

After first period, Monica takes her time gathering her things. I wait for her outside the classroom. She hesitates when she sees me and then tries to duck around. I block her way.

"Please give me a chance to explain! I feel terrible," I say.

"Not now!" Monica snaps. "I don't want detention for being late to Ms. Feeny's English class."

I can't argue with that. I step aside. "Fine. I'll see you at lunch!"

Monica just hurries away. I don't know if she heard me. Maybe she just doesn't care.

I can't stand the thought of losing Monica. I don't want to lose Brad, either—even if I am mad.

I catch him at his locker. He doesn't run when he sees me. He stops and glares. That just makes me madder!

Why is Brad acting like I'm the bad guy? I'm not the one who broke my promise and wrecked Monica's life.

Okay, well, I did—sort of. I told Brad. But Brad told the world!

I lift my chin, turn, and stomp away.

· CLAUDIA ·

CHAPTER 11

Monica

I'm having a terrible day.

I'm mad at Claudia. But I also feel bad about ignoring her.

And I miss Rory so much. We haven't talked in days. I've been too afraid to call him or text him. I just know he heard the rumor and is angry with me. Planning on breaking up with me. Maybe in his mind he already has.

And I'm embarrassed to walk down the hall. I wish someone had asked me to explain my side of the story. Nobody did. Not even Chloe.

That stung. We've been best friends for over two

years. Chloe should know I wouldn't do anything to hurt Rory. I'm not mean or stupid, and I care about him a lot.

Chloe's waiting in our English class. She looks at me and points to the empty seat beside her.

I walk over, but I don't sit down. "Are you still mad? Are you going to yell at me or something?" I say quietly.

"No, I want to apologize," Chloe says. "I should have asked you if the rumor was true."

"Of course it's not true," I say. I sit down.

"I know." Chloe sighs. "I almost called you last night, but I wanted to apologize in person. I got here too late to catch you in homeroom."

"Where were you?" I glance at Ms. Feeny. If we're still talking when the bell rings, we'll both be staying late after school.

"I missed the bus," Chloe explains. "Mom drove all the way back home from the hospital to give me a ride."

"So how did you find out it wasn't true?" I ask, but the bell rings, so she doesn't answer.

Chloe writes something in her notebook and turns it so I can see.

Lunch.

I nod. I'm glad Chloe knows I'm innocent. I just wish Rory thought so, too. Having Chloe on my side gives me hope, though. Rory might listen to her.

After class, Chloe and I part ways until 4th period science. After science, we walk to the cafeteria together.

"How did you know I didn't cheat on him?" I ask.

"I couldn't figure out why you'd risk losing Rory for a weekend fling," Chloe explains. "Then I realized. You wouldn't."

"You're right about that," I say.

Chloe nods. "You're not a cheater, and you adore Rory. I never should have doubted you."

After we get our food, I look for Rory, but he's

not in the cafeteria. Once we sit down, I tell Chloe the whole Eric story.

"In a weird way, the rumor is true," I say.

"No, it's not," Chloe says. "That creep kissed you, and you pushed him away. That's not cheating."

"I'm glad you understand," I say. Then I sigh and add, "I just wish Rory did."

"What do you mean?" Chloe asks. "Why doesn't he understand that?"

"Rory hasn't talked to me or called since that rumor started," I say. "He wasn't at lunch yesterday, and he's not here today. He's avoiding me. Plus, the other day as he was going into geometry, I tried to talk to him and he didn't want to talk to me."

"That doesn't sound like Rory." Chloe pokes at her veggies. "He wouldn't believe a rumor without giving you a chance to explain."

"You're one of my best friends, and you did," I say.

"I know, but only until I stopped to think about

it," Chloe says. "Rory really likes you. There's got to be another reason he hasn't been around."

I shrug. "Then why hasn't he called me?"

Chloe looks me in the eye. "Ask him."

I shake my head. "I can't. What if—"

Chloe leans forward. "You have to ask him. If you don't, you'll be assuming the worst without giving him a chance to explain."

Chloe has a point. I owe it to Rory to ask.

* * *

He doesn't show up for 7th period study hall again. I sit alone.

Claudia sits alone.

Brad sits alone.

On the bus ride home, I try to text Rory. But every message I think of sounds ridiculous.

I want to just forget this whole thing ever

happened. I want to go back to the day before I left for Viv's house and tell my mom I changed my mind. I want to go back to Saturday and tell Eric I'm too tired to go to the movies. I want Eric to stop being a total jerk and to not have kissed me.

When I get home, I change into jeans and riding boots. Then I hop on my bike and head for Rock Creek Stables.

Rory works at the barn after school when he doesn't have football or basketball or baseball practice. If my ambush fizzles and he won't let me explain, I can pretend I'm there to ride. Or actually ride. I haven't even seen Lancelot, the horse Chloe's mom lets me ride, in weeks.

I usually like the bike ride between my house and the barn almost as much as I like riding Lancelot on the trails. The bike path cuts through the park. The trees are shady, the gardens are full of flowers, and everyone is having fun.

Today I feel so down that it doesn't even seem pretty.

My brain buzzes with what I want to say to Rory.

When I get to the stable, Mark, the trainer, is giving a riding lesson in the main ring. I wave as I pedal down the drive. He walks over. "Hey, Monica! I haven't seen you in a while. How are things?"

"Really good," I say, trying to sound casual. "Is Rory here?"

Mark points to a barn. "He's cleaning stalls."

Rory is working in the first stall. He looks up when I walk in. He's wearing an old t-shirt and scruffy jeans, but he still looks gorgeous. My breath catches in my throat when I look into his big, brown eyes.

I blurt out a frantic explanation. "I don't know what you heard, Rory, but it isn't true. Well, not exactly. I mean, I didn't cheat on you."

Rory arches an eyebrow and just stares at me.

I keep babbling. Of course. That's what I do when I'm upset. "I told Eric I had a boyfriend," I say, my voice getting higher and higher. "But he tricked me into going to the movies anyway. He said his friends were going to be there. Anyway, he didn't try anything during the movies, so I thought he had gotten the message, but he didn't. I wasn't paying attention and he kissed me. I didn't want it to happen. It just did."

Rory nods and leans the pitchfork against the stall. I fight back tears. I wonder if being honest was a mistake. I just confessed to kissing another boy! I'm so upset, I turn to leave.

Rory jumps to stop me. "Monica, wait! Where are you going?"

"I don't know," I say. I exhale slowly, trying to compose myself. "I just can't stand seeing you so mad at me."

"Mad?" Rory shakes his head. "What do you mean? I'm not mad."

"You're not?" I ask, confused.

"No!" He smiles at me. "I didn't believe that stupid rumor."

"You didn't?" I say. "But—"

"I feel terrible that you thought I was mad at you," Rory says.

But I still don't get what's been going on. "If you weren't mad at me, why have you been avoiding me?" I ask.

"I'm not avoiding you." Rory shakes his head and grins. "Not at all, actually. My geometry teacher has been tutoring me during lunch and study hall. The rest of the time I've been at basketball practice or cramming for midterms."

I'm relieved that Rory knows the truth about the kiss, but now I feel like a jerk.

"I am so sorry," I say. Tears spring to my eyes. "I should have known you wouldn't believe a bunch of gossip. You're smarter than—"

"Shut up and come here." Rory folds me in his arms and gives me a kiss. "If that Eric creep didn't live so far away, I'd rush over to his place right now and defend your honor."

That makes me smile, but it quickly fades. I look down again.

Rory frowns. "What else is wrong?" he asks.

"I don't know if I'm angrier at Claudia for telling Brad about the kiss or angrier at Brad for telling you," I say.

"He didn't tell me," Rory says. "I heard it from some other guys. And none of them heard it from Brad."

That doesn't make me feel better. If Brad didn't start the rumor, Claudia did.

· MONICA ·

CHAPTER 12

CLAUDIA

For the past two days, the hot topic at school has been the Monica-cheated-on-Rory rumor. But by the time I get to my locker on Thursday, nobody's mentioned it. I cross my fingers. If everyone stops talking about it maybe Monica will talk to me again!

I feel even more hopeful when I see Monica and Rory walking ahead of me. They're holding hands.

I get a huge rush of warm, happy feelings. Followed by a big dose of sad.

Rory obviously let Monica explain what happened with Eric. Then they made up.

That won't work for Brad and me. Brad broke a really important promise. There's no excuse for that.

Rory gives Monica a quick hug at our homeroom door and moves on. I try to catch Monica before she sits down, but I'm not fast enough. Monica sits with Chloe and Tommy. They huddle with their heads together, talking.

She's probably telling them how she and Rory worked things out.

That makes me sad again. I want to fix this with Brad! I love him, and I hate fighting.

Anna walks in and slides into the chair next to me. "Guess what," she says.

"Monica and Rory made up," I say. "I know."

"That's great!" Anna says. "But that's not what I found out."

"What did you find out?" I ask.

"Well, like I said, I knew Brad didn't spill the beans about that dude kissing Monica," Anna says.

"So I asked a bunch of kids who told them the rumor. Using my detective skills, I was able to track the rumor to the real big mouth."

"It wasn't Brad?" I ask.

"No. It was Karen Chen," Anna says. "She was in the girls' restroom when Monica told you about Eric."

I frown. "No way," I say. "We looked to make sure no one else was in there."

"I know," Anna says. "Karen was sitting with her feet up so nobody could find her. Her boyfriend was home sick, and they were texting."

"Why was she hiding out to do that?" I ask.

"Karen's friends are nosy," Anna says, rolling her eyes. "They always want to read her texts, and she just wanted some privacy."

I'm still confused. "Okay, but if Karen heard us, why did she tell everyone Monica cheated?"

"She only heard parts of what you said," Anna explains.

"The bad parts," I say.

Anna shrugs. "I guess, but it's all good now. Rory and Monica are okay, and the true story will get around eventually."

It's not all good.

Monica and Brad are still mad at me, and they both have good reasons. Maybe Anna's new info will help me patch things up.

I don't have another class with Monica until lunch, but I can catch Brad in the computer lab.

Yesterday Brad got to class first and sat between Adam and Larry. I didn't care. I was mad so I didn't want to talk to him, either.

Today I have to apologize.

I walk as fast as possible without getting yelled at and wait outside the classroom door. When Brad walks up with Adam, I block the doorway and start talking. "I'm sorry I accused you of starting the rumor about Monica, Brad—"

"You're in the way, Claudia," Brad says.

"But I have something to tell you!" I struggle to stay calm. Other kids are piling up behind Brad and Adam.

"I hope you're not charging admission," one kid jokes.

"I'm not paying to get in," another kid says.

"Is there a problem out there?" Mr. Lopez asks loudly.

"We have to talk," I tell Brad as I move aside.

"No, we don't." Brad doesn't look at me as he walks by.

I take a few deep breaths. I feel like crying, but I don't. I've never given up on anything, and I'm not going to give up on this.

One way or another, I'll make Brad listen to what I have to say.

And hope he understands and forgives me.

* * *

At lunch, I decide to wait until he sits down. Then he can't walk away. Besides, Anna will be there to back me up.

But Brad doesn't sit at our usual table. He sits with the basketball team.

I have to tell Brad that I'm a stupid girl who should have believed her boyfriend and didn't. I don't want to do it in front of seven other guys! But I don't have a choice.

I psych myself up as I walk to the table. Apologizing in front of the team might help. Then Brad will know for sure that I'm super, sincerely sorry.

Another boy notices me first. He nudges Brad. When Brad looks back, I go for it.

"I know you're mad at me, Brad, and you have every right to be. I was wrong and stupid and—"

"Okay, Claudia. Can I eat now?" Brad turns back to his lunch.

My cheeks burn as I turn away.

Being rudely humiliated in front of the team is horrible, but there's something worse.

Rory cared enough to let Monica explain.

Brad won't listen to anything I say. He's acting like a guy who is breaking up with his girlfriend and just hasn't told her yet.

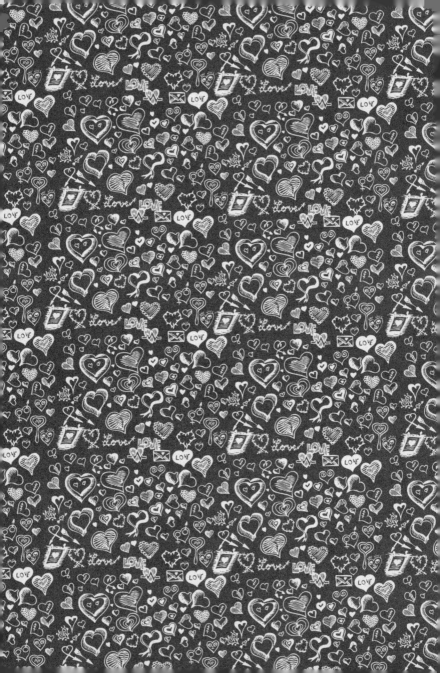

CHAPTER 13

Thank goodness I have Chloe.

All of my so-called friends, or most of them anyway, are pretending I don't exist. They don't know what to say or they think I did something wrong. I hate it the most when other girls giggle, point, and whisper. They don't do it behind my back. They want me to know they're talking about me.

Chloe and I go to lunch together. Nobody else is sitting at our usual table.

"Where is everyone?" Chloe asks as we slide into seats.

"Rory has a tutoring session with Mr. Johnson," I say. I cast a quick glance around the cafeteria. "Brad is sitting with the basketball team again."

I see Claudia walking toward us. I haven't spoken to her in two days. She passes the team table without looking at Brad. He doesn't look at her, either. She sits down across from us. I look down at my food.

"Hi, Claudia," Chloe mumbles.

"I know how the rumor got started," Claudia blurts out. "It wasn't me or Brad."

I can't ignore that! "Who was it?" I ask.

"Karen Chen," Claudia says.

"Who told her?" I ask.

"You did," Claudia says.

"No, I didn't!" I exclaim, shocked. "You're the only one I told, Claudia."

"Karen was in the bathroom, in a stall, with

her feet up," Claudia explains. "She heard you tell me what happened with Eric, but she didn't hear everything. She thought you said you cheated on Rory."

"It wasn't you!" I say. I laugh. "You have no idea how happy I am to hear that!"

"Does that mean you're not mad at me anymore?" Claudia asks.

Before I can answer, Chloe jumps in. "If you knew Monica hadn't cheated on Rory, why didn't you say so?"

"I did!" Claudia exclaims. "I sent you a text yesterday morning."

"Oh." Chloe turns a little red. "I deleted all my texts. I was sick of reading bad jokes about Monica."

"I stopped reading texts, too," I say. "They were too depressing."

Claudia exhales in frustration. "I figured everyone would pass it on. If they are, it's not setting any speed records." She sighs. "Sorry I made such a mess of things, Monica."

"It's not your fault Karen was eavesdropping in the girls' room," I say.

"I know, but I promised I wouldn't tell anyone," Claudia says. "I told Brad, and seriously, Monica, you don't know how much I wish I hadn't."

"Brad didn't start the rumor," I say. "You thought you could trust him, and you were right." I'm still a little annoyed that Claudia told Brad, but I'll get over it. I just want to patch things up with my best friend and move on.

"Are you and Brad fighting?" Chloe asks.

Claudia nods. "It's my fault. Brad swore he didn't tell anyone Monica's secret, and I didn't believe him. Now he's so mad he won't let me explain or apologize."

"Brad has to talk to you if you're helping him with his English essay," I say. I'm so glad my friends know that I'm not a cheater. I don't want anyone else to be sad. Especially Claudia.

"I don't know if he still wants my help," Claudia says. "And I can't ask him if he won't talk to me."

"Text him," I suggest.

"What if he doesn't read it?" Claudia asks.

"What if who doesn't read what?" Anna asks as she and Carly sit down.

Claudia quickly explains the problem.

"Boys can be such brats!" Anna says, rolling her eyes. "Send the text. If he doesn't read it, at least you tried. Then if he flunks out of basketball, he can't blame you."

"Besides," I add. "He might read it and accept."

"I guess it can't hurt to try." Claudia reads as she types: "I'm still willing to help you with English, if you still want my help."

"Perfect!" Anna says, smiling. "Direct and straight to the point."

"Here goes nothing," Claudia says. She taps the screen.

We all watch Brad. He looks at his phone and

frowns. He hesitates, but then he reads the message and types.

Claudia's phone beeps.

"What did he say?" Anna asks. She leans over to look, and reads the text out loud. "Okay. When and where?"

"My house, 7 o'clock tonight," Claudia says, typing a response. She sends the text, but her face is worried. "What if Brad won't accept my apology?"

"You have to think positively," I tell her.

Chloe smiles. "And you have to remember that you guys love each other. You can make it work!"

"I hope you're right," Claudia says. "But I think I really screwed things up for good this time."

CHAPTER 14

CLAUDIA

It's 6:57. I pace in the front hall. I can't sit still. In fact, I'm kind of freaking out. I'm glad everyone in my family is gone, because I know they'd all be wondering what's up with me.

What if Brad doesn't show up?

I peek out the window. There's still no sign of him, but it's not 7 o'clock yet. I go into the living room, sit down on the couch, and jump up again.

I really am losing it.

What if Brad shows up, but he won't listen to my apology?

What if he listens to it, but he won't accept it?

What if he doesn't show up?

What if this is it?

What if it's over?

Just as I'm sure he's not going to come, the doorbell rings.

I tell myself to think positive, like Monica said. Brad and I can get through this. We love each other. We're perfect for each other.

Then I count to three, calm down, and open the door. "Hi," I say. I smile. Just looking at him makes me start to feel better.

He doesn't smile. "Hey," he says. He walks in, but he doesn't go to the living room and flop on the couch like he usually does. He stands in the hall and shifts his weight from one foot to the other—like a stranger.

That's when I realize how ridiculous this whole thing has been. A few days ago, nothing could have come between me and Brad. We thought we'd be together forever. How can we let this rip us apart?

"I'm going to help you, like I promised," I say. "But first, I have something to say."

Brad looks at his feet. "I really don't—"

I cut him off. "I should have believed you when you told me you didn't break your promise about Monica's secret. I know you didn't, and I'm sorry."

Brad looks at me. "Why are you so sure of that now?" he asks.

"Karen was in the bathroom, even though we thought it was empty. She heard Monica tell me about Eric. She started the rumor," I explain. "So I know it wasn't you!"

I give him a big smile, trying to show how happy I am to be talking to him again. But he doesn't smile back.

"So you needed proof," Brad says. "You can't just believe that I'd never tell someone a secret you told me. Especially a secret about your best friend. Especially something really hurtful or something that you were worried about."

"I was sure nobody else knew," I whisper.

"You should have given me the benefit of the doubt anyway," Brad says.

"I know," I say.

"I mean, what kind of guy do you think I am? Honestly, Claudia, I thought you knew me better than that," he goes on. He's really angry, and his ears are starting to turn red. "That's not who I am."

I sigh and nod. "I know."

"Well, I'm glad you know I wasn't lying and that I didn't break my promise," Brad says. "But that doesn't mean everything is okay."

"What do you mean?" I ask quietly. Tears are forming in my eyes.

"I'm not sure I want to be with a girl who doesn't trust me." Brad tightens his jaw. "I have to go," he adds, and before I can say anything, he's gone.

I cry myself to sleep.

· CLAUDIA ·

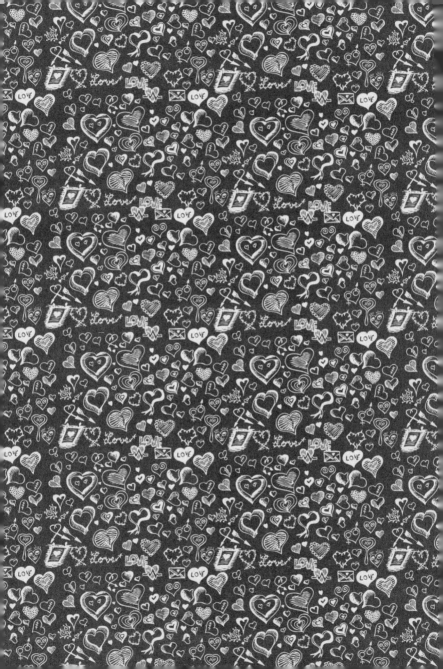

CHAPTER 15

Monica

As soon as Chloe and I walk into homeroom on Friday morning, I know something's wrong.

Claudia's sitting by herself, doodling in a notebook, looking miserable. And Brad, looking just as miserable, is sitting by himself on the other side of the room.

"I guess Brad is still mad," I say when I sit down.

"I guess," Claudia says with a sigh.

"But he's talking to you, right?" Chloe asks.

"Not really," Claudia says. "He told me that he doesn't know if he can be with someone who doesn't trust him."

I'm shocked. Claudia and Brad are the perfect couple, and everyone knows it.

"What's his problem?" I ask. "I thought for sure that you'd make up after you explained everything."

She shrugs. "I guess not. I guess this was just unforgivable."

As soon as the bell rings, I corner Brad in the hallway. He won't talk to her, but he might listen to me.

"Got a minute?" I ask.

"Not really," he says. "I've got to get to science."

"Well, this won't take long," I say.

He ducks into an alcove, and I follow. "What's up?" he asks.

"You know what's up," I say, crossing my arms. "You're making my best friend miserable."

Brad shakes his head. "Yeah, and what she's been doing to me for the last four days has been really awesome," he says. "Stay out of it, Monica."

"I can't," I say. "This whole thing with you and Claudia started because of me."

"Not really," he says. "It started because Claudia decided she couldn't trust me."

"I want to explain something," I say. "Before I told Claudia that creepy Eric guy kissed me, she swore she wouldn't tell anyone else." I hold his gaze. "For me, that meant anyone, including you."

"And she broke her word," Brad says.

"Yes," I agree. Then I go on. "But only because in Claudia's mind, you didn't count. You're not just anyone to her. You're her boyfriend."

"Right," Brad says. "The guy she thinks is a liar."

I shake my head and quickly get to the point. "Claudia broke my trust, but I didn't want to lose her as a friend over it. I let her explain. She was wrong, but she was also very upset and sorry about it. And I understand why she told you. She's upset and sorry about what happened with you, too."

"I know," Brad says.

"But you're still mad," I say.

Brad shrugs. "Some things are too big to get over."

"Are you sure this is one of them?" I ask.

"Being thought of as untrustworthy by the girl I thought loved me as much as I loved her?" he says. "Yeah, that's big enough to not get over."

"What about from her point of view?" I say.

"What do you mean?" he asks.

"Not being forgiven even after realizing you were wrong and apologizing. And losing the person you love more than anything," I say gently. "That's her point of view."

Then I walk away. I don't know if it'll make a difference, but I hope at least it gave him something to think about.

I'm a few minutes late to algebra, but Mr. Palmira knows I'm a good student, and he lets me slide in without saying anything.

"Where were you?" Claudia whispers when I sit down next to her.

"Talking to Brad," I say.

Claudia looks hopeful. "Were you talking to him about me?" she asks.

"Yeah, but . . . I don't think it did any good," I say.

"That's too bad." Claudia's voice trembles a tiny bit. She clears her throat. "But thanks for trying."

"No problem," I say gently.

Claudia looks down at her paper. Then she looks at me, and I see tears in her eyes. "I don't understand why this isn't bothering him," she says. "Why it's so easy to let me go, over something so stupid. Such a stupid mistake."

"I know," I whisper. "I'm sorry, Claudia."

We don't talk much after that. And in study hall, Brad's not there. Neither is Rory, but I knew that already—he's getting geometry tutoring again.

I want to talk to Claudia, try to make her feel better, but I can tell she doesn't feel like thinking about Brad. Besides, we both want to get as much homework done as possible before the weekend.

* * *

After school, Rory is waiting at my locker to give me a ride home. "Hey!" I say, wrapping my arms around him. After all the drama with Claudia and Brad, I'm glad we can have a few minutes of just-us time. I've missed it. "How was your tutoring?"

"Good," he says quietly. He seems a little troubled. Off, somehow.

"What's up?" I ask. "Are you okay?" I put my things in my locker and grab my coat.

We start to walk down the hall. "Yeah, I guess," he says.

"Something's on your mind," I say. We head into the parking lot, and I take his hand. "What is it?"

"I don't like getting into other people's business," Rory begins. "But the split between Claudia and Brad is really bugging me."

"How come?" I ask. Rory is more sensitive than most boys, but he still doesn't like drama.

"Brad isn't the greatest basketball player, but he's better than half the guys on the team," Rory explains. "And he's been totally off his game the past few days."

I take my hand away.

"Wait. You're worried about it because you're worried about the team?" I say. "What about Claudia? She's utterly miserable. Brad's skills on the court are the least of my worries right now."

Rory looks shocked as we get into the car. "That's not what I meant," he says. "I'm worried about my friend. For something to bug him enough to screw up his game, it's got to be big. This is really bothering him."

I grab his hand again. "I'm sorry," I say. "I shouldn't have snapped at you. I guess it's bothering all of us, and I can't figure out how to fix it."

"I don't even know the whole story," Rory says, pulling the car out of the parking lot. "Fill me in?"

Oh yeah. Boys don't discuss relationships. "Okay," I say. "Claudia thought Brad told someone else about the whole Eric thing," I explain.

Rory's nostrils flare when I mention Eric's name, but he doesn't say anything, so I keep talking. "When the rumor started, the evidence did point to him. I only told Claudia, and she only told Brad. We didn't know Karen heard part of what I said, so we had no idea it was her who spread the rumor. So when Brad swore that he didn't tell anyone, Claudia didn't believe him."

"Did Claudia admit she was wrong and apologize?" Rory asks.

"Yes, of course," I say. "But the damage was totally done by that point. Brad thinks she should have trusted him in the first place so he's still mad."

"He's got a point," Rory says.

"I know, but they like each other so much," I say.

"I know," he says. "They're basically the perfect couple." Then he looks over at me, winks, and squeezes my hand. "Not as perfect as us, of course," he adds.

"Do you think they can get through this?" I ask.

Rory smiles. "I hope so," he says. "After all, you kissed another guy and I forgave you—"

I yank my hand away. "Rory!" I say. "I didn't kiss—"

"Relax, cutie," he says, grinning. He pulls the car to a stop at a red light. "I was just joking." Then he leans over and gives me a long, deep kiss.

I melt into his arms, and we're still kissing when suddenly a bunch of cars start honking. The light has changed, and we're holding up traffic.

"Whoops," he says, smiling. "Worth it."

I laugh. "Definitely," I say.

"You make me really happy," he says. "I'm glad we're cool. I'm really glad we're not Brad and Claudia right now."

"What would you do if you were Brad and I was Claudia?" I ask.

Rory thinks for a minute. "I'm not sure," he says. "Feeling like that—like you didn't trust me—that would be horrible."

"I know," I say quietly.

"But everyone makes mistakes," Rory says. "Eric did, by messing with my girl. You made a mistake, by not just telling me about him right away so I could tell you to stop worrying. Claudia did, by telling Brad, and then by assuming he'd been the one to spill the beans."

"You're right," I say.

"And Brad will make a huge mistake," Rory goes on. "If he lets Claudia get away."

I nod.

"So I guess I hope if I were in his shoes, I'd figure that out," Rory says, resting his hand on my leg. "Because if I had to choose between forgiving you for something that wasn't that big of a deal, or losing you forever?" He shakes his head. "Well, I hope I never lose you. So I hope Brad realizes that too, about Claudia."

"I wish he saw it that way," I say.

"I think he will," Rory says. "I really do."

CHAPTER 16

CLAUDIA

After dinner on Friday night, all I want to do is sit on the couch. That's the only good thing about being home alone on a Friday night. It's been a ridiculously terrible week, and next week might be worse. I need something to take my mind off of everything.

I pick up the remote and flick through the channels.

But even with two hundred channels and tons of movies on demand, I can't find anything I want to watch. My mind keeps wandering back to Brad.

What's he doing right now? Is he going out? With the guys? Where? What if he meets someone else?

My phone beeps. I have a text from Anna.

Want to go see The Third Charm?

Who's going? I write back.

Me and Carly. We're meeting Trace and Tyler after.

Anna and Carly are just friends with Trace and Tyler—for now. Still, I don't want to be the pathetic odd girl out.

I'm sure Anna has noticed that Brad is avoiding me, and she probably wants to pick my brain. She's very good at it, and I'm not ready to explain anything.

Thanks, but I've got plans.

Really? OK.

I can tell that Anna doesn't believe me, but it's not a lie. I plan to stay home, watch TV, and eat popcorn while I'm feeling sorry for myself.

Just then, the doorbell rings. I know it's not

for me, so I don't move from the couch. I just keep flicking through the channels.

The bell rings again. Twice.

"Answer the door!" Dad yells from the kitchen.

"Okay!" I roll my eyes. Then I walk to the front door and fling it open, a grumpy look on my face.

Brad is standing on my front porch.

My stomach churns, my hearts flutters, and my mind whirls. I can only think of two reasons why Brad would come to see me tonight.

He wants to make up. Or he wants to break up for good.

"What are you doing here?" I ask.

"Will you read this essay?" Brad asks. He hands me a sheet of paper. "To see if I'm on the right track."

All of my romantic ideas fly out of my head. The ideas about how this is him begging me to stay with him.

Clearly, this is just about homework. I promised

to help him pass the English midterm, and reading what he writes is part of the job.

"Um, sure," I say. "Come on in."

Brad follows me into the living room. He sits on one end of the sofa, and I sit on the other.

The title of his essay is "The Trouble with Pride."

"Great title," I say.

"It's based on that old saying 'Pride cometh before a fall,'" Brad says.

I assume he wrote about sports. Then I read the first two lines: *Friends should trust each other. Friendship—and love—can't last without trust.*

It's obvious that Brad wrote about us. I don't look at him as I read on. He doesn't mention names, but he explains what he did right and I did wrong: Person A promises not to tell a secret. The secret leaks out, and Person B thinks Person A talked— even though Person A swears he didn't.

I take a deep breath and hope Brad doesn't

notice. The essay is written fine, and it doesn't need my help. He clearly just wanted to rub it in, keep making me feel miserable and guilty. I can't believe he wants to hurt and humiliate me like this!

I certainly don't want him to know that it's working.

I keep reading.

Next Brad points out that Person B realized she was wrong and apologized.

Then he asks: *Is that enough? Should Person A forgive and forget?*

I read the next sentence and gasp.

The answer is—yes!

I look up at Brad. "Yes? Does this mean you forgive me?"

"Yeah," Brad says. He shifts position and ends up sitting a little closer. "Keep reading."

This time, I read out loud. "'If Person A is too stubborn to swallow his pride, he will lose Person

B. She's the best friend he ever had and the only girlfriend he ever wants, and he loves her very much.'"

I'm so overwhelmed I can't talk. Tears—this time, of happiness—crowd my eyes.

"Is it stupid?" Brad asks.

"No, it's perfect," I say.

"Does that mean you'll forgive me?" he asks.

"Forgive you?" I ask. "For what?"

"For almost letting you go just because I felt hurt and insulted," he explains.

"Are you serious?" I grin. "Of course I forgive you."

Brad squeezes my hand and kisses me. "Good. Because Monica and Rory are on their way over to get us. We're all going to the Rafters."

"We are?" I look down at my ratty old sweatshirt and jeans. Then I jump up. "Don't move. I'll be right back."

"I'm not going anywhere," Brad says with a smile. "Ever."

THE END

About the Author

Diana G. Gallagher lives in Florida with five dogs, four cats, and a cranky parrot. Her hobbies are gardening, garage sales, and grandchildren. She has been an English equitation instructor, a professional folk musician, and an artist. However, she had aspirations to be a professional writer at the age of twelve. She has written dozens of books for kids and young adults. Her bestselling Claudia Cristina Cortez and Monica books are available from Stone Arch Books.